For Hugh

Scholastic Canada Ltd.
604 King Street West, Toronto, Ontario M5V 1E1, Canada

Scholastic Inc.
557 Broadway, New York, NY 10012, USA

Scholastic Australia Pty Limited
PO Box 579, Gosford, NSW 2250, Australia

Scholastic New Zealand Limited
Private Bag 94407, Botany, Manukau 2163, New Zealand

Scholastic Children's Books
Euston House, 24 Eversholt Street, London NW1 1DB, UK

www.scholastic.ca

Nick used acrylic paint on paper to create these illustrations.
Typeset in Geist Serifa.

Library and Archives Canada Cataloguing in Publication

Bland, Nick, 1973-, author, illustrator
The very sleepy bear / [written and illustrated by] Nick Bland.

Originally published: Gosford, NSW : Scholastic Australia, 2017.
ISBN 978-1-4431-6334-7 (hardcover).--ISBN 978-1-4431-6335-4 (softcover)

I. Title.

PZ7.B557Ves 2018   j823'.92   C2018-900099-6

First published by Scholastic Australia in 2017.
This edition published in Canada by Scholastic Canada Ltd. in 2018

6 5 4 3 2 1   Printed in China LFA   18 19 20 21 22

The VERY SLEEPY BEAR

NICK BLAND

Scholastic Canada Ltd.

Toronto New York London Auckland Sydney
Mexico City New Delhi Hong Kong Buenos Aires

Winter had come early and Bear was running late.
He was feeling very sleepy, it was time to hibernate.

He hurried down the mountain, past the icy rocks,
and never even noticed a rather sneaky Fox.

At last he reached his cozy cave
just in time for bed,
then Fox appeared from nowhere:
"Good afternoon!" he said.

"I couldn't help but notice that your cave is very small.
There's hardly any room in here to hibernate at all!
A great big bear like you," said Fox, "so big and strong and brave,
a creature so magnificent . . . deserves a bigger cave."

"A bigger cave? For me?" yawned Bear.
"Perhaps you could be right.
I must admit this little cave
is getting rather tight."

"Today's your lucky day!" said Fox.
"I've just the cave for you!
I'll even help you pack," he said.
"I've nothing else to do."

So Bear picked up his suitcase
and he gave a little wave.
And left his cozy home behind
to find a bigger cave.

"Forget your little cave,"
said Fox.
"This **huge** one
could be yours!
There's heaps of room
to hibernate!
It's even got two doors.

It's absolutely waterproof,
free from snow and rain,
and once a day at two o'clock
you get to see . . .

Fox was smiling nervously
and Bear just shook his head.
"I'm feeling very sleepy.
I'm going home," he said.

"But you're so very big," said Fox,
"and your cave, so very small.
You really need a **bigger** cave,
a cave that's nice and . . .

. . . tall!

This one's made of solid wood,
and not a train in sight!"

"And never mind the bats," said Fox, "they all go out at night."
Fox was smiling nervously and Bear just shook his head.

"I'm feeling very sleepy.
I'm going home," he said.

"**But wait!** There is another cave
if that one's not for you."

"It's got a sandy floor," said Fox,
"and a lovely ocean view!"

"I'll take it!" said the sleepy bear,
and shook the fox's hand.
He took his favourite pillow out
and curled up in the sand.

But just as Bear was nodding off
inside his brand-new cave,
there came a splishy
splashy sound
and then there came . . .

Bear was cold and cranky
and very, very tired.
He packed his little suitcase up.
"I'm going home!" he sighed.

When Bear arrived back home at last, ready for his bed,
Fox and all his little friends were living there instead!

"**Please** don't throw us out," said Fox. "We're all so very small.
You'll hardly even notice that we're living here at all."

"Well, today's your lucky day,"
said Bear as he lay upon the floor.

"Wake me up in spring," he said,
"and by the way . . .

. . . I snore."

ZZZZ
ZZZZZ
ZZZZZ